Mel opened the cage so Lily could walk in, then called the little pup. Coco turned when he heard his name, and Lily saw his floppy ears and deep brown eyes. Then he turned back to his bowl. Only once he'd finished every last bit did he trot over to see Lily.

Mel laughed. "He was very underweight when he came in to us, so we had to feed him up. Now he's turned into a bit of a greedy pup!"

Tim laughed as the tubby little dog rolled over to have his tummy tickled. Lily was hesitating – she wanted to stroke Coco, but she hung back. Noticing, her big brother looked up at her. "Come on, Lily, he wouldn't hurt a fly," he reassured her.

Lily crouched down, and Coco rolled over and gave her a big doggy grin. "He's smiling!" she gasped.

D1428726

www.randomhousechildrens.co.uk

www.battersea.org.uk

Have you read all these books in the
Battersea Dogs & Cats Home series?

COCO's
story

by
Sarah Hawkins

Illustrated by Sharon Rentta
Puzzle illustrations by Jason Chapman

RED FOX

BATTERSEA DOGS & CATS HOME: COCO'S STORY
A RED FOX BOOK 978 1 849 41908 6

First published in Great Britain by Red Fox
an imprint of Random House Children's Publishers UK
A Random House Group Company

This edition published 2011

1 3 5 7 9 10 8 6 4 2

Copyright © Random House Children's Books, 2011
Illustrations copyright © Sharon Rentta, 2011
Additional illustrations copyright © Jason Chapman, 2011

All rights reserved. No part of this publication may be reproduced, stored in
a retrieval system, or transmitted in any form or by any means, electronic,
mechanical, photocopying, recording or otherwise, without the prior
permission of the publishers.

The Random House Group Limited supports The Forest Stewardship Council
(FSC®), the leading international forest certification organisation. Our books
carrying the FSC label are printed on FSC® certified paper. FSC is the only forest
certification scheme endorsed by the leading environmental organisations,
including Greenpeace. Our paper procurement policy can be found at
www.randomhouse.co.uk/environment

MIX
Paper from
responsible sources
FSC® C016897

Set in 13/20 Stone Informal

Red Fox Books are published by Random House Children's Publishers UK,
61–63 Uxbridge Road, London W5 5SA

www.**randomhousechildrens**.co.uk
www.**totallyrandombooks**.co.uk
www.**randomhouse**.co.uk

Addresses for companies within The Random House Group Limited
can be found at: www.randomhouse.co.uk/offices.htm

THE RANDOM HOUSE GROUP Limited Reg. No. 954009

A CIP catalogue record for this book is available from the British Library.

Printed and bound in Great Britain by
CPI Group (UK) Ltd, Croydon, CR0 4YY

Meet the stars of the
Battersea Dogs & Cats
Home series to date

**Turn to page 93 for lots
of information on
Battersea Dogs & Cats Home,
plus some cool activities!**

Meet the stars of the Battersea Dogs & Cats Home series to date . . .

Bailey

Misty

Chester

Rusty

Max

Daisy

Snowy

Stella

Angel

Huey

Alfie

Cosmo

Coco

Battersea Dogs & Cats Home

"I'd like a Border collie," Lily's brother Tim said excitedly. "Or a German shepherd. They're so smart, the police train them to catch burglars." Lily's tummy turned over anxiously as she listened to her brother. "Do you think they'll have Border collies, Mum?" Tim continued. "My friend Michael's got one and it knows loads of tricks."

"We'll just have to wait and see what dogs they have," Mum replied patiently. "I'm sure the perfect dog will be there waiting for us."

Lily and Tim were in the car with their parents on the way to Battersea Dogs & Cats Home, to find a dog of their very own! Lily was excited, but she was also very, very nervous. Some of the breeds that Tim was talking about grew very

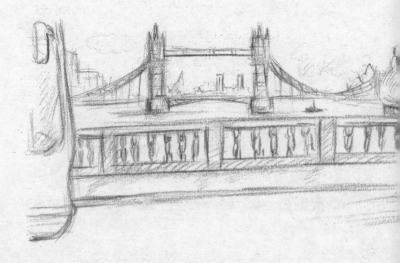

large, and Lily was a bit scared of big dogs. There was one living a few doors down from their house that always leaped up at the gate and barked when she passed, and it made her jump every time.

Secretly, Lily would have preferred a rabbit, or something small and fluffy that she could cuddle. But she knew Tim had always wanted a dog, and she did want one too . . . as long as it wasn't too big . . .

Tim must have
noticed her looking
worried because he
squeezed her
hand. "Don't
worry, Lily, we'll
get a friendly
dog. Besides,
he'll be *our*
dog, so he won't
bark at you – he'll
smother you with
licks!"

Lily smiled, but her tummy lurched
again as Dad parked in a nearby street
and they all walked up to the entrance of
the Home. Lily stared up at the big glass
building to their right, then gasped as she
saw a cat peering out of each of the
windows! "Look, Mum!" she cried.

"Oh yes!" Mum laughed. "They're looking out for the families who are coming to adopt them."

Lily wasn't so sure. She thought they looked a bit snooty, gazing down on everyone coming in, and wondering who they were. She edged behind Mum as they walked past the cattery into the reception.

"Oh, Lily, you're scared of everything!" Mum sighed. "Come on, let's go and find a lovely little puppy.

Maybe if you're not the baby of the family any more you'll be a little bit braver!"

They walked into the reception and were met by a friendly- looking lady. "Hello!" she said. "I'm Jenny. Let's go and have a chat so I can find just the right pet for you!"

Jenny took them into a little room, which had a computer and a few chairs in it.

But one of the chairs
was already taken
– there was a
huge golden
retriever
lolloping on it!
"Oh, Roger, what
are you doing in

here?" Jenny laughed. She turned to Lily
and explained, "That's Roger. He belongs
to one of our staff and he's not really
supposed to be here!
Come on, out you
go!"
Lily jumped
back as Roger
came past, but
the golden-yellow
dog just wandered
out into the corridor,

looking as if he owned the place. Lily couldn't imagine taking her dog to work, but it seemed like everyone at Battersea loved dogs so much they didn't mind having Roger around!

They told Jenny that they were looking for a puppy and she asked them all about their house and garden, and how much time they spent at home. "Puppies can't be left on their own as much as adult dogs," she told them, "so someone needs to be home for most of the day, at least until they're grown up."

"That's OK," Tim said eagerly. "I can stay at home with him!"

"Er, what about school?" Dad asked, raising an eyebrow.

"Well, if the puppy needs me, then I don't mind not going to school," Tim declared.

The adults all laughed. "Thanks, Tim, but I'll be at home anyway, so that won't be necessary." Mum smiled as Tim sighed. "I work part-time as a receptionist," Mum explained to Jenny, "so I only work mornings. I'll be home in the afternoon. And we've got lots of willing volunteers to take him out for walks in the evenings. We'll need your help then, Timmy," she said. "And yours, Lily," she added.

Mel smiled at Lily kindly. "Yes, you've been very quiet, Lily. Would you like to come and see some adorable puppies?"

Lily nodded shyly and Jenny led them through into the kennels. As soon as the door opened, all the dogs started barking and Lily's heart began to beat fast. They might be tiny, but these puppies had VERY big barks . . .

Coco the Chocolate Brown Labrador

Lily hid behind Dad as they went into a
narrow hallway with cages on either side.
In every one was a fully grown dog, not
a puppy after all, and it seemed to Lily
like each dog she passed was bigger
than the last! One of them leaped up
at the wire mesh, and Lily jumped
back in fright.

"Don't worry, petal." Dad put his arm around her. "They're just excited, they don't want to hurt you. Look!" The dog that had jumped up was grinning at them with his tail wagging excitedly. "He's friendly really."

"Hello, boy!" Tim was rushing from pen to pen greeting all the dogs. He wasn't scared at all. Lily looked at the huge dog, and he gave another loud bark.

But this time it didn't sound as though he was saying "I want to eat you"; it was more like a noisy "Hello!"

"Hello," Lily said shyly.

"The puppies are through here," Jenny shouted over the noise. "They've just been given their dinner, so they should be nice and quiet!"

She showed Lily and her family through to another kennel. Sure enough, the only sound was eager munching and the occasional happy "Yip!"

Tim rushed off again, racing to the cage at the end of the row. "Cool!" he shouted out excitedly. Lily crept closer to the nearest enclosure and peeked in. She could see a dog basket with something furry curled up inside, a few chew toys scattered around and a food bowl. A tiny puppy had his nose so far into the bowl that all Lily could see of him was a little brown bottom and a tail that was wagging happily from side to side!

"These are our chocolate-brown Labrador pups. That's Coco," Jenny said, pointing at the bottom with a smile. "And the little girl curled up in the

basket is his sister Candy. We've already found a nice family for Candy, but Coco's still looking for his for-ever home. Do you want to go and meet him?"

Lily nodded shyly. Jenny opened the cage so Lily could walk in, then called the little pup. Coco turned when he heard his name, and Lily saw his floppy ears and deep brown eyes.

Then he turned back to his bowl. Only once he'd finished every last bit did he trot over to see Lily.

"Cool!" Tim cried again, bursting into the cage and skidding down onto his knees. Coco put his head on one side and looked at Tim curiously as he reached out to stroke him.

"Here, boy," Tim called. Coco rushed over to his hand and sniffed it.

"He's probably looking for some more food!" Jenny laughed. "He was very underweight when he came in to us, so we had to feed him up. Now he's turned into a bit of a greedy pup!"

Tim laughed as the tubby little dog rolled over to have his tummy tickled. Lily was hesitating – she wanted to stroke Coco, but she hung back. Noticing, her big brother looked up at her. "Come on, Lily, he wouldn't hurt a fly," he reassured her.

Lily crouched down, and Coco rolled over and gave her a big doggy grin. "He's smiling!" she gasped.

"He likes you!" Tim told her. "Here, stroke him behind his ears." Lily touched his velvety ears and the soft, warm patch of skin behind them, and Coco wagged his tail in delight.

Lily stretched over to touch his tail, and Coco suddenly jumped up. She flinched, but Coco just put his front paws on her lap, then started nuzzling into her middle. "What's he doing?" Lily giggled.

"I think he's smelled something in your pocket. Have you got any food in there?" Jenny asked.

Lily reached into the pocket of her jumper and brought out a squashed bit of chocolate. Coco jumped about excitedly, and gave a little whine. Lily looked into his big brown eyes. They were just like chocolate drops! "Oh, is that why he's called Coco?" she realized.

Jenny nodded. "But I'm afraid you can't give him that. Human chocolate can be poisonous for dogs – even chocolate-brown Labs! And besides," she said, leaning down to ruffle Coco's ears, "you've had enough to eat today, you little piggy."

"He'd probably eat us out of house and home," Dad laughed.

Lily reached out to touch Coco's soft fur again. He was the cutest puppy she'd ever seen. Suddenly she wanted a puppy desperately, more than she'd ever wanted anything else in her life.

"Tim eats a lot and we keep him!" she exclaimed.

"Don't you want to look at the other puppies?" Mum asked, giving Candy a tickle under the chin. "Chocolate Labs do grow quite big, you know . . ."

Lily glanced at Coco. The roly-poly pup was poking his little brown nose around his bowl to check that he hadn't missed any food. He snuffled under the empty bowl and tipped it over, then gobbled up a tiny chunk of meat. Then he came over to Lily and plonked himself down in front of her, ready for another tummy-rub. Lily knew that Coco would never try and frighten her. He was as gentle and fluffy as a rabbit – but much, much better!

She shook her head. "Coco's the one I want."

"Me too," Tim added, stroking the puppy protectively.

Mum looked at Tim and Lily's faces and gave a laugh. "You two look as desperate as Coco did when he was after that chocolate!" she joked. "It must be a perfect match!"

Coco Comes Home

"Thank you, Tim, but there's no need for you to miss school," Mum said with a smile.

It was a week since they'd met Coco, and the nice lady from Battersea Dogs & Cats Home had been round to visit their house and check that it would be a good place for Coco to live. Tim had shown her their garden, where there was plenty of

room for Coco to
run around. Lily
had shown her
the big basket
in the corner of
the kitchen where

Coco was going to sleep.

Mel had told them it all looked lovely,
and that she was sure Coco was going to
be very happy with them. Best of all, she
had said that they could pick him up as

soon as they were
ready!

Now it was
Monday morning,
and Tim was
desperate to go
with Mum to bring
Coco home instead
of going to school.

Lily wanted to go too, but she was nervous about not going to school. Miss Bourner was very strict, and Lily didn't think she'd be very happy if she went to Battersea instead of to her lessons – even if it was to get the cuddliest puppy ever!

"No more arguments, Tim," Mum said firmly. "You're going to school and that's that. I'm going to fetch Coco. He can settle in at home this morning, and then Dad and I will bring him to pick you up this afternoon. And if you don't put your uniform on right this minute, then you'll be going to school with your pyjamas on."

Tim got dressed pretty quickly after that, but he moaned all the way to school, and when Lily saw him in the playground at lunchtime he complained that the day was going really slowly.

Lily spent the whole day feeling excited and anxious. She hoped Coco was OK and hadn't been too frightened by the journey home. It must be really scary being a little puppy and leaving a lovely place like Battersea, where everyone looks after you. *But you're going somewhere even better*, she thought. *You're going to be with a family of your very own who will love you for ever!*

As soon as the home-time bell went, Tim burst into Lily's classroom. "Come on, Lily, hurry up!" he yelled, "Mum and Dad are outside with Coco!" Lily shoved her books into her backpack higgledy-piggledy and raced after her brother.

Her parents were in the playground
with the tubby little brown puppy sitting
at their feet. Coco was even more round
and cuddly than the last time they'd seen
him! Lily rushed over to stroke him, and
Coco jumped up to sniff at her backpack.

"I've still got some of my sandwich left, Mum, can I give it to him?" Lily asked.

"No," Mum said, "I've got some doggy treats for him. But we have to be careful not to feed him too much – the lady at Battersea said he was getting a bit too chubby!"

"Aw, he's perfect!" Lily smiled, stroking Coco, who immediately flopped onto his back so that she could rub his tummy.

"Well, give him a treat each, and then we'll walk home though the fields and let him run it off," Mum said, handing both Tim and Lily a dog biscuit.

Coco smelled the snacks straight away and started jumping up at Lily's legs, his tail wagging wildly as he snapped at her closed fist. If it had been any other dog, Lily would have been frightened that it was going to bite her, but she knew Coco only wanted the food!

She put her
hand out
flat, and
Coco gently
took the
treat from
her palm.
Lily
squealed as
she felt his soft
wet mouth on her
hand, and wiped his dribble down her
school trousers.

"Oh, Lily!" Mum said disapprovingly.

"Oops, sorry!" Lily smiled.

Tim held his treat up high in the air so
Coco had to leap up for it. The tiny
puppy was so determined to get the food
that he jumped up as high as he could,
his tail wagging excitedly.

"Whoa!" Dad cried as Coco hurled himself upwards. "Have we brought home a puppy, or a baby kangaroo?"

Tim finally gave Coco the treat and the puppy dropped it on the floor and crunched it up. Then he looked up eagerly, as if to say, "Can I have some more?"

When Tim shook his head and said, "Sorry, boy," Coco turned to Lily and gave a small whine.

"No more!" Lily said, holding up her hands to show him they were empty. "But it's time for a walk!" She grinned, bending down to stroke Coco's soft head.

Tim got to hold Coco's lead first, and Lily walked next to the tiny puppy, on the road-side. Normally she liked to stay on the inside of the pavement, away from the cars, but she didn't want Coco to be frightened as the traffic whizzed past. Dad smiled and said how pleased he was that Lily was being so responsible.

When they got to the stile that led over to the fields behind the village, Tim sped away, calling, "Coco, come on, boy, come on!" The little dog plodded after him, pulled along by his lead.

Tim wrenched a twig off a nearby bush and threw it, but Coco just looked at it, then sat himself down at Tim's feet. Tim ran over and picked up the stick to try again. "Fetch!" he yelled as he threw it across the field. Coco watched as the stick soared away, then gave a yawn.

Tim sighed, gave Coco's lead to Mum to hold, and jogged over to pick the stick up again.

Lily giggled as she ran to join them.

"Isn't the dog supposed to go and get the stick?" she laughed. Tim gave a roar, and chased her instead.

Lily squealed and ran away, with Coco gambolling along next to her. "Coco, save me!" she shrieked.

"Woof!" Coco replied, but instead of chasing Tim he plonked

himself down on his bum and sat there, panting happily.

"Oh, Coco!" Lily cried, throwing herself down next to him and giving him a hug. Tim sat down on Coco's other side. Mum came over and took a picture of them with her phone.

"You all look so cute together." She smiled.

"Coco's part of the family already!" Lily grinned, kissing his soft brown head.

A Mud Monster!

"Come on, we'd better head home," Mum said after a while, passing Lily the lead.

"It's been a very exciting day for such a young puppy!" said Dad.

But Coco didn't want to go. The naughty pup raced away, pulling the lead out of Lily's hand.

"*Now* he wants to run around!" Tim joked.

As Tim bent down to grab him, the
puppy darted to the side and dodged
about all over the place, thinking that
this was a new game. He bent
down and rested on his front
paws, with his bum and
tail in the air.
"Woof!" he said.
*"Come on,
chase
me!"*

"Come on, Coco," Lily called. "It's time to go home for dinner."

That got Coco's attention! He raced straight towards Lily – right into a big patch of mud. Coco lifted his paws up and stared at them, looking very surprised. His paws were even darker brown now that they were coated in mud! He touched his nose to the dirt and whined pitifully.

"Oh no!" Lily gasped. Poor Coco!
"Mum! Dad! Coco's stuck in the mud!"
she yelled as she raced over to her
parents, who had been walking ahead.
She pulled Dad over to where Coco was
standing miserably in the middle of the
dirt. He was looking very sad indeed.

"Oh, Coco!" Mum sighed. "Tim, you'd better get him out."

"Can I?" Tim grinned. Mum always moaned when he got his clothes muddy.

"Yes, just this once," Mum said reluctantly. "We'll put your uniform in the wash as soon as we get home."

Tim ran full pelt into the muddy puddle. Coco's tail wagged as he got closer, and he barked happily when Tim scooped him up, and held him against his chest to wade back to the others.

Mum sighed when she looked at Tim's dirty shoes and trousers. When he put Coco down, she groaned again. There were muddy paw prints all over Tim's school shirt!

Lily felt sorry for Coco – it didn't seem as though he'd enjoyed that at all: he looked like a tiny swamp monster! Coco shook himself and splattered Tim with even more mud. Her brother didn't seem to mind.

"For once you can't blame me for making a mess!" Tim said happily. "It was Coco the mud-brown Labrador!"

When they got home, Mum made Tim and Coco stand in the front garden while she went to fetch the garden hose. She attached it to the warm tap in the kitchen sink, then unravelled it through the house and out of the front door.

"Here you go, Lily!" she laughed. "Do you want to spray your brother and your troublemaker puppy for me? Give me a shout when you're ready and I'll turn the tap on."

"Yes, please!" Lily giggled.

"You're enjoying this waaay too much!" Tim said.

"Don't fight or I'll make it the *cold* tap!" Mum called from the kitchen.

"OK, OK!" Tim grumbled. Mum turned the tap on, and a jet of water shot out of the hose. Coco yelped excitedly and batted the end with a paw. Tim picked up the squirming pup, and Lily came closer to direct the warm water onto his muddy paws.

Even his tail was coated in thick brown sludge. Lily gently rubbed him until the mud came out of his fur, getting herself quite wet in the process.

"There now, doesn't that feel better?" she asked. Coco looked up at her with his chocolate-drop eyes and licked her nose with his tiny pink tongue. "Woof!" he barked happily.

Mum had put some towels on the front doorstep, so Lily and Tim bundled up the dripping puppy and rubbed him all over. Coco loved the attention and snuggled so deeply into the towel that all Lily could see was his nose and his tail poking out.

Once he was dry – and looking extra
fluffy – Lily popped him safely inside with
Mum and Dad and turned to her brother.

"Oops, looks like we used up all the
hot water on Coco," she said with a
wicked grin as she pointed the hose right
at Tim . . .

The Secret Weapon

Once Tim had taken a hot bath and he and Lily were both in their pyjamas, everyone sat down at the dining-room table to eat their dinner. It was spaghetti bolognese, Lily's favourite – and it looked like it might be Coco's favourite too! The little pup was sitting by her feet, staring at her like he hadn't been fed in a month!

Lily twisted the spaghetti round her fork, but as she moved it to her mouth she noticed the puppy's gaze following her. He looked so sad that Lily couldn't concentrate on her dinner. "Can't he just have a little bowl of spaghetti bolognese?" She asked. "It would be just like in *Lady and the Tramp!*"

"No," Dad said firmly. "He's had enough of his own food, so he can't be hungry, he's just being greedy. We can't feed him too much – it's very bad for dogs to get fat."

Lily bent down and stroked Coco's head. "Sorry," she whispered as the pup whined, "but you're not allowed any."

Coco slunk away with his tail between his legs – but went straight round to where Tim was sitting and started begging from him!

"No, Coco," Tim said, but when he thought Mum and Dad weren't looking he slipped a piece of the long pasta under the table. Coco rushed over to gobble it up.

"OK, that's it," Mum said, jumping up from the table.

"I dropped it!" Tim protested. "Spaghetti is

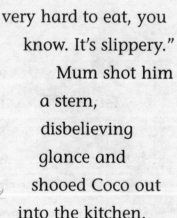

very hard to eat, you know. It's slippery." Mum shot him a stern, disbelieving glance and shooed Coco out into the kitchen.

"You can stay in here until we've finished," she told him. "And if you're good you can have some doggy treats later." Coco's ears pricked up at the word "treats", but he lay down sadly when Mum started to close the kitchen door.

Lily felt really bad that Coco was shut in the kitchen, but her plump little pooch definitely had eyes bigger than his tummy and needed to learn not to be so greedy!

*

Lily always went to ballet classes after school on Tuesday, so it was late when she arrived home the next day. As soon as she got in the front door she called Coco. He came running out, looking very excited to see her, and Lily bent down to give him a cuddle. "Did you miss me, Coco?" she whispered into his fur. "I missed you!"

Then she noticed her brother looking bad-tempered.

"What's wrong?" Lily asked.

"I've been trying to teach Coco tricks all evening," Tim grumbled. "And he just won't do anything I want. Look!"

Lily put Coco down and Tim sat next to him.

"*Coco, sit,*" Tim said, pressing his hand down gently on the top of Coco's bum.

Coco looked at Lily and grinned as if it was all a big joke, then walked away and started sniffing round the kitchen door. Mum was in there cooking dinner – and Coco was much more interested in the delicious smells coming from the kitchen than obeying Tim's commands!

"I've got an idea!"
Lily cried. She
rushed into the
kitchen and
opened the
cupboard
where Coco's
food and treats
were kept. She
put a handful of
treats in her pocket
and hid one in the
palm of her hand, curling her fingers
over so that it was out of sight. "Hi,
Mum," she called innocently as she ran
back into the lounge.

"I bet Coco will do whatever I want!"
Lily boasted to her brother. It looked like
Coco could already smell the treats,
because he'd wandered away from the

kitchen door and was
sniffing round
Lily curiously.
Lily crouched
down next to
him.

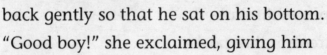

   "*Coco, sit,*"
she said in a firm
voice, pushing his
back gently so that he sat on his bottom.
"Good boy!" she exclaimed, giving him

the treat. Coco
gobbled it
eagerly, and
Lily put
another one in
her fist. When
he'd finished it,
Coco looked at
her expectantly.

"Sit," Lily said, holding her breath. Coco sniffed at her closed hand, nuzzling it to try and get at the treat inside. "*Sit, Coco*," Lily said again.

Coco plonked himself down on his bum. "Good boy!" Lily laughed, giving him the treat. "Look, Tim, he did it. I taught him a trick!"

"How did you do that? I've been trying for ages!" Tim groaned.

"I've got a secret weapon," laughed Lily, pulling the treats out of her pocket and showing them to Tim. "Coco will do *anything* to get his paws on some food!"

"Woof!" Coco agreed, poking his nose into her pocket and munching noisily.

A Big Dog and a Little Bunny

When it was time for their dinner Tim and Lily went to sit at the table, and Mum shut Coco in the kitchen again. All through their meal they could hear Coco whining and scratching at the door. "He must be hungry, Mum," Lily insisted. "He sounds like he's *starving*!"

Tim nodded, looking as worried as Lily.

"Honestly he's not, darling," Mum said gently. "He's had more than enough food today. And you've just given him a whole load of treats! I saw what you were up to. He'll soon learn that he's not allowed our dinner and then he won't make such a racket."

"Tell you what, let's take him out for a walk after dinner," Dad suggested. "Running about should take his mind off his tummy!"

As soon as she'd finished, Lily leaped down from the table and went into the kitchen to comfort Coco. She clipped his lead onto his collar, and was standing at the front door with her coat on before Dad had even finished his pudding!

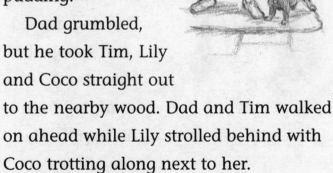

Dad grumbled, but he took Tim, Lily and Coco straight out to the nearby wood. Dad and Tim walked on ahead while Lily strolled behind with Coco trotting along next to her.

Lily was feeling so happy that she

forgot to cross the road like
she usually did before
she reached the house
with the red gate. As
she passed it, the
huge dog that lived
there threw himself
up against the gate,
barking frantically.

Lily jumped back in
fright and
burst
into tears. The
big dog snarled
and snapped at
her, drool
hanging from
his mouth. He
gave a low
rumbling growl.

"Arf!" came a reply. Coco was
standing in front of Lily, barking
his tiny puppy bark at the
huge dog that
towered over
him.

Lily scooped up the puppy and
rushed after the others. "Coco, you're so
brave!" She smiled through her tears. "If
you're not scared of that big dog, then I
won't be either. Although you shouldn't
fight with him – he's big enough to eat
you for breakfast."

Coco's tail wagged at the word "breakfast". "Oh, you funny pup!" Lily cried. "Do you ever think of anything apart from your tummy?"

By the time they got to the wood, Lily had forgotten all about the big dog. The leaves were just starting to turn orange and yellow, and the wood was full of colour. Lily held on tightly to Coco's lead, and the little dog trotted along next to her as she walked, wandering off every now and again to follow an interesting smell.

Dad and Tim were still up ahead, having a chat about trains. Lily hung back to wait for Coco, who had disappeared into a patch of thick bushes. All she could see was his plump chocolate-brown tail, which was wagging happily.

"What are you doing in there, Coco?" Lily said out loud. "Coco!" she called, but he didn't appear. She started to feel a bit nervous. What if there was a snake or something in the bushes that had hurt her puppy? She called again, sounding a bit cross because she was worried. Coco still didn't come out. Lily's tummy twisted but she swallowed her fear. If Coco wouldn't come out – then she'd just have to go in!

"Coco," she shouted, pushing aside some thorny branches and peering inside. As her eyes adjusted to the gloom she could see Coco crouching next to a patch of blackberries. He had blackberry juice all over his nose and was looking *very* pleased with himself.

"Oh, Coco!" Lily laughed. "You're so naughty, and SO greedy! How can you fit so much food in that tiny body?!"

Coco wriggled forward on his belly and reached out to grab another berry with his teeth.

"No," Lily said in a warning tone. Coco looked at her and gave a little whine. "No, Coco," she said firmly. "You'll get a bad tummy." She grabbed the 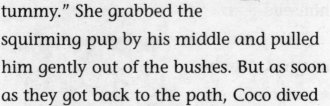 squirming pup by his middle and pulled him gently out of the bushes. But as soon as they got back to the path, Coco dived back in again.

"Coco!" Lily cried.

Lily tried to grab him again, but Coco just wriggled out of reach, further into the prickly bushes.

The prickles didn't
seem to hurt Coco's
furry coat, but a
thorn made a
long scratch
down Lily's arm
as she tried to
pull him onto
the path.

Lily was just
wondering if she'd
ever get Coco out when
a flash of brown caught her eye. The
naughty pup had disturbed a rabbit.
Coco gave a "Yip" as he saw the rabbit
too. Before Lily could move, he was
tearing out of the bushes after the bunny.
Lily had never seen him move so fast! He
raced past Tim and Dad, but the rabbit
was quicker, and disappeared into

another patch of
brambles.
Coco sat
down for a
rest.

"You'll
have to get
a bit fitter if
you want to
catch a
rabbit," Tim told
him.

"He obviously prefers his food to be
stationary," Dad joked, "and brought to
him in a bowl!"

Coco tried to look as if he'd never
wanted to catch the rabbit anyway, and
trotted back towards the blackberry bush.

"Oh no you don't!" Lily laughed and
picked him up. "You've had enough.

Besides, if you get any chubbier I won't be able to lift you up and give you a hug!" She smiled as Coco snuggled into her arms happily. "I don't want you to get any chunkier OR any skinnier," Lily said as she hugged him tight. "I love you just the way you are!"

Coco the Hungry Hero

Lily spent Saturday morning watching cartoons on the sofa with Coco, trying to keep him away from her bowl as she ate her cereal. Tim sat on the floor, throwing a ball against the wall.

"No, Coco!" Lily said for the hundredth time. "Just because they're called *Coco Pops* does not mean they're for you!"

"Morning, guys," Mum said with a yawn as she came into the lounge. "I was thinking that we could go over to Auntie Jo's house today. We can take Anna her birthday cake, and I'm sure she'd love to meet Coco."

"Oh yeah!" Lily exclaimed. She loved spending time with her auntie and her cousin, and she'd never had anything as cool as Coco to show them! Lily ran upstairs to get dressed, then brushed Coco's fur with the soft dog brush Mum had bought for him. Coco loved the attention, and wriggled and squirmed on Lily's lap in delight as she brushed his fur until it shone. "You are the handsomest puppy in the world!" Lily said, kissing him on the top of his soft head.

They'd just left the house when Mum cried, "Oh drat, I forgot Anna's cake. You guys carry on slowly and I'll catch you up."

Tim and Lily carried on round the corner, but just as Lily was walking over the zebra crossing, Coco spotted something.

Lily suddenly heard a tinkling, ringing sound. Heading straight for her was a cyclist, shouting angrily and ringing his bell. Lily didn't know whether to keep going or turn back. She froze with fear and closed her eyes tight. The cyclist was going to hit her!

Coco suddenly pulled on his lead, jerking Lily forward – and the cyclist rode by where Lily had been standing seconds earlier! She landed with a thump on the pavement, and Tim came rushing over.

"Coco saved your life!" he said in amazement.

"Lily!" came a shout from across the road. Mum ran over and knelt down next to Lily. "That cyclist shouldn't have done that," she said angrily. "You were on the crossing. You could have been really hurt. Are you OK?" she asked as she checked Lily's hands and knees for scrapes and bruises.

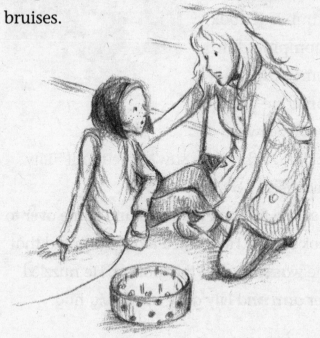

"Coco pulled me out of the way just in time!" Lily said.

"Do you think he saw the cyclist?" Mum wondered.

Lily looked over at the puppy, who was standing nearby with his head in a hamburger box, chomping down some chips that someone had thrown away.

"No, I think he saw some food!" Lily laughed.

Coco finished the chips and came over to look at Lily. He seemed really surprised that she was sitting on the ground. He nuzzled her arm and Lily gave him a big hug.

"No one can tell you off for being a greedy pup now," she said smiling. "Your hungry tummy saved the day!"

"Yes, you can have an extra-large dinner tonight!" Mum laughed.

"And pudding!" Tim added, stroking Coco behind the ears.

But Coco wasn't listening. He was sniffing Anna's birthday cake curiously . . .

Read on for lots more . . .

🐾 🐾 🐾 🐾

Battersea Dogs &
Cats Home

Battersea Dogs & Cats Home is a charity that aims never to turn away a dog or cat in need of our help. We reunite lost dogs and cats with their owners; when we can't do this, we care for them until new homes can be found for them; and we educate the public about responsible pet ownership. Every year the Home takes in around 10,500 dogs and cats. In addition to the site in southwest London, the Home also has two other centres based at Old Windsor, Berkshire, and Brands Hatch, Kent.

The original site in Holloway

History

The Temporary Home for Lost and Starving Dogs was originally opened in a stable yard in Holloway in 1860 by Mary Tealby after she found a starving puppy in the street. There was no one to look after him, so she took him home and nursed him back to health. She was so worried about the other dogs wandering the streets that she opened the Temporary Home for Lost and Starving Dogs. The Home was established to help to look after them all and find them new owners.

Sadly Mary Tealby died in 1865, aged sixty-four, and little more is known about her, but her good work was continued. In 1871 the Home moved to its present site in Battersea, and was renamed the Dogs' Home Battersea.

Some important dates for the Home:

1883 – Battersea start taking in cats.

1914 – 100 sledge dogs are housed at the Hackbridge site, in preparation for Ernest Shackleton's second Antarctic expedition.

1956 – Queen Elizabeth II becomes patron of the Home.

2004 – Red the Lurcher's night-time antics become world famous when he is caught on camera regularly escaping from his kennel and liberating his canine chums for midnight feasts.

2007 – The BBC broadcast *Animal Rescue Live* from the Home for three weeks from mid-July to early August.

Amy Watson

Amy Watson has been working at Battersea Dogs & Cats Home for six years and has been the Home's Education Officer for two and a half years. Amy's role means that she organizes all the school visits to the Home for children aged sixteen and under, and regularly visits schools around Battersea's three sites to teach children how to behave and stay safe around dogs and cats, and all about responsible dog and cat ownership. She also regularly features on the Battersea website – www.battersea.org.uk – giving tips and advice on how to train your dog or cat under the "Fun and Learning" section.

On most school visits Amy can take a dog with her, so she is normally accompanied by her beautiful ex-Battersea dog, Hattie. Hattie has been living with Amy for just over a year and really enjoys meeting new children and helping Amy with her work.

The process for re-homing a dog or a cat

When a lost dog or cat arrives, Battersea's Lost Dogs & Cats Line works hard to try to find the animal's owners. If, after seven days, they have not been able to reunite them, the search for a new home can begin.

The Home works hard to find caring, permanent new homes for all the lost and unwanted dogs and cats.

Dogs and cats have their own characters and so staff at the Home will spend time getting to know every dog and cat. This helps decide the type of home the dog or cat needs.

There are three stages of the re-homing process at Battersea Dogs & Cats Home. Battersea's re-homing team wants to find

you the perfect pet: sometimes this can
take a while, so please be patient while
we search for your new friend!

1 Register details

2 Match

3 Leaving with your new pet

Have a look at our website:
**http://www.battersea.org.uk/dogs/
rehoming/index.html** for more details!

"Did you know?" questions about dogs and cats

- Puppies do not open their eyes until they are about two weeks old.

- According to *Guinness World Records*, the smallest living dog is a long-haired Chihuahua called Danka Kordak from Slovakia, who is 13.8cm tall and 18.8cm long.

- Dalmatians, with all those cute black spots, are actually born white.

- The greyhound is the fastest dog on earth. It can reach speeds of up to 45 miles per hour.

- The first living creature sent into space was a female dog named Laika.

- Cats spend 15% of their day grooming themselves and a massive 70% of their day sleeping.

- Cats see six times better in the dark than we do.

- A cat's tail helps it to balance when it is on the move – especially when it is jumping.

- The cat, giraffe and camel are the only animals that walk by moving both their left feet, then both their right feet, when walking.

Dos and Don'ts of looking after dogs and cats

Dogs dos and don'ts

DO

- Be gentle and quiet around dogs at all times – treat them how you would like to be treated.
- Have respect for dogs.

DON'T

- Sneak up on a dog – you could scare them.
- Tease a dog – it's not fair.
- Stare at a dog – dogs can find this scary.
- Disturb a dog who is sleeping or eating.

- Assume a dog wants to play with you. Just like you, sometimes they may want to be left alone.
- Approach a dog who is without an owner as you won't know if the dog is friendly or not.

Cats dos and don'ts

DO

- Be gentle and quiet around cats at all times.
- Have respect for cats.
- Let a cat approach you in their own time.

DON'T

- Never stare at a cat as they can find this intimidating.

- Tease a cat – it's not fair.
- Disturb a sleeping or eating cat – they may not want attention or to play.
- Assume a cat will always want to play. Like you, sometimes they want to be left alone.

Some fun pet-themed puzzles!

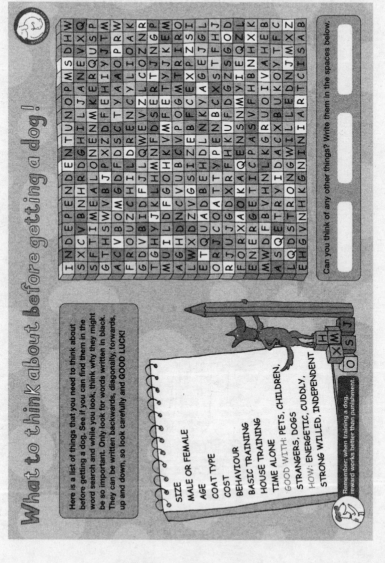

What to think about before getting a dog!

Here is a list of things that you need to think about before getting a dog. See if you can find them in the word search and while you look, think why they might be so important. Only look for words written in black. They can be written backwards, diagonally, forwards, up and down, so look carefully and GOOD LUCK!

SIZE
MALE OR FEMALE
AGE
COAT TYPE
COST
BEHAVIOUR
BASIC TRAINING
HOUSE TRAINING
TIME ALONE
GOOD WITH: PETS, CHILDREN, STRANGERS, DOGS
HOW: ENERGETIC, CUDDLY, STRONG WILLED, INDEPENDENT

Remember: when training a dog, reward works better than punishment.

Can you think of any other things? Write them in the spaces below.

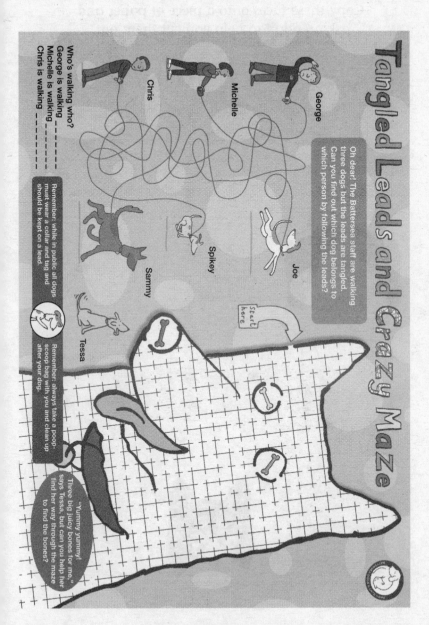

Tangled Leads and Crazy Maze

Oh dear! The Battersea staff are walking three dogs but the leads are tangled. Can you find out which dog belongs to which person by following the leads?

Chris

Michelle

George

Spikey

Joe

Sammy

Tessa

Who's walking who?
George is walking – – – – – – – –
Michelle is walking – – – – – – – –
Chris is walking – – – – – – – – – –

Remember: while in public all dogs must wear a collar and tag and should be kept on a lead.

Remember: always take a poop-scoop bag with you and clean up after your dog.

Start here

"Yummy yummy! Three big juicy bones for me," says Tessa, but can you help her find her way through the maze to find the bones?

108

Making a Mask

Copy these faces onto a piece of paper and
ask an adult to help you cut them out.

Here is a delicious recipe for you to follow.

Remember to ask an adult to help you.

Cheddar Cheese Dog Cookies

You will need:

227g grated Cheddar cheese

(use at room temperature)

114g margarine

1 egg

1 clove of garlic (crushed)

172g wholewheat flour

30g wheatgerm

1 teaspoon salt

30ml milk

Preheat the oven to 375°F/190°C/gas mark 5.

Cream the cheese and margarine together.

When smooth, add the egg and garlic and mix well. Add the flour, wheatgerm and salt. Mix well until a dough forms. Add the milk and mix again.

Chill the mixture in the fridge for one hour.

Roll the dough onto a floured surface until it is about 4cm thick. Use cookie cutters to cut out shapes.

Bake on an ungreased baking tray for 15–18 minutes.

Cool to room temperature and store in an airtight container in the fridge.

There are lots of fun things on the
website, including an online quiz, e-cards,
colouring sheets and recipes for making
dog and cat treats.

www.battersea.org.uk